BOXER AND BRANDON

D1285000

www.kidkiddos.com

Copyright©2015 by S. A. Publishing ©2017 by KidKiddos Books Ltd.

support@kidkiddos.com

Second edition, 2019

Library and Archives Canada Cataloguing in Publication
Boxer and Brandon
ISBN: 978-1-5259-1492-8 paperback
ISBN: 978-1-77268-391-2 hardcover
ISBN: 978-1-77268-067-6 eBook

KidKiddos Books

Created by Inna Nusinsky

Illustrations by Gillian Tolentino

Hello, my name is Boxer. I'm a boxer.

No, not one of those fighting guys with the red gloves—I'm a type of dog called a boxer. Nice to meet you!

Well, this is the story of how I got my new family.

It all started when I was two years old. You're probably thinking that two is really young, but that's like 14 in dog years!

I was homeless. I lived on the street and ate out of garbage cans. People got pretty mad at me when I knocked over their trash cans.

"Get out of here!" they would shout. Sometimes I had to run away really fast! Living in the city can be hard.

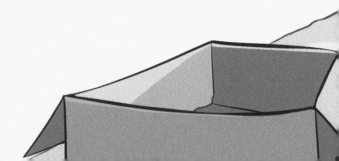

When I wasn't looking for food, I liked to sit and watch people walk by on the sidewalk.

Sometimes, I would look at people with my sad eyes and they would give me food.

"Oh, what a cute doggy! Here, have a snack," they would say.

One day, a little boy and his dad were walking toward me. The boy looked like he was about eight years old. That's really old in dog years!

"How's that peanut butter and jelly sandwich, Brandon?" asked the boy's dad.

It looked really good!

I put on my sad eyes. The boy stopped and held out his sandwich.

I was just about to take a bite, when...

"Brandon, don't feed that dog! He'll just come looking for more," exclaimed his dad. Brandon pulled the sandwich back.

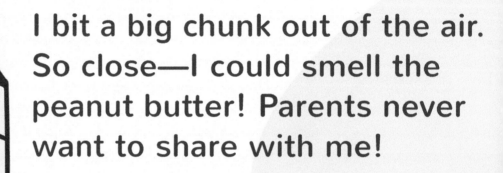

I bit a big chunk out of the air. So close—I could smell the peanut butter! Parents never want to share with me!

I whined as pitifully as I could as they walked away.

After that, I decided to chase a cat, and then I took a nap.

I was having a wonderful dream. I was in a park and everything was made from meat—the grass was bacon! The trees were steaks!

It was the best dream ever.

Something woke me up, though. Right in front of me was a piece of a sandwich!

I jumped to my feet and gobbled it down. Mmmmm! It was so good! It had bacon and steak, just like my dream.

"Shh," said Brandon. "Don't tell Dad." What a nice little boy, I thought to myself.

Day after day, Brandon would come visit me and give me a snack. It was the best!

Then, one day...

"Hurry up, Brandon. You'll be late for school," said Brandon's dad.

"I'm coming!" shouted Brandon as he ran past.

He dropped a brown bag on the sidewalk.

Sniffing around, I walked up to it and looked inside. It was full of food! My mouth was watering.

I was just about to eat it all when I thought of something. *Brandon always brings me food when I'm hungry.If I eat his food, then he'll be hungry. That isn't fair.*

"I'm coming, Brandon!"
I howled.

He and his dad were way down the street. I ran after them with the brown bag in my mouth.

As I was passing an alleyway, I saw a cat. I hate cats! I forgot about my mission and dropped the bag.

"Bark, get out of here, cat! Bark, bark!" I barked.

Then I remembered Brandon's lunch. He was going to be hungry if I didn't bring him his lunch!

It was hard, but I forgot about the cat. I picked up the brown bag again and started running.

Further down the street, I stopped again. A butcher shop!

There were pieces of meat and sausages hanging everywhere.

Mmmmm...Wait! I had to bring Brandon his lunch or he was going to be hungry!

It was hard, but I forgot about
the meat. I grabbed the lunch
and started running again.

I turned a corner and stopped. There was another dog wagging his tail.

"Hi, want to play?" he woofed.

"I sure do!" I answered. "Oh, wait, I can't right now. I have to bring Brandon his lunch. Did you see a little boy with his dad?"

"Yep, they went that way," he barked, and pointed with his nose.

It was hard, but I forgot about playing. I grabbed the lunch and started running again.

I could see the school—and there was Brandon with his dad!

I ran as fast as I could. Stopping in front of Brandon, I dropped his lunch bag on the sidewalk. Just in time!

I was breathing hard and my tongue was sticking out.

"Look, Dad, he brought my lunch!" exclaimed Brandon.

"That's amazing!" said his dad.

They both patted me on the head.

Brandon was happy and so was his dad.

In fact, his dad was so happy that he brought me home. He gave me a bath. He gave me food! He even gave me a bed to sleep in.

Now when Brandon and his dad go walking, I get to walk with them. And when they go home, I get to go home with them!

I love my new home and my new family!

CPSIA information can be obtained
at www.ICGtesting.com
Printed in the USA
BVHW020801140620
581478BV00004B/192

9 781525 914928